FOR BRIAN CROUCHER AND ALL OUR ADVENTURES. ONWARDS, MY FRIEND!

Henry Holt and Company, LLC
Publishers since 1866
115 West 18th Street
New York, New York 10011

Henry Holt is a registered trademark of Henry Holt and Company, LLC

First published in the United States in 2000 by Henry Holt and Company, LLC
Distributed in Canada by H. B. Fenn and Company Ltd.
Originally published in Great Britain in 1999 by Frances Lincoln Limited.

Library of Congress Cataloging-in-Publication Data
Balit, Christina
Atlantis: the legend of a lost city: adapted and retold from
Plato's Timaeus and Critias / by Christina Balit; with a note by
Geoffrey Ashe.
Summary: Recounts the legend of the lost civilization of
Atlantis. Includes a note discussing various explanations for
the legend.
[1. Atlantis—Juvenile literature. 2. Atlantis.] I. Plato.
Timaeus. English. II. Plato. Critias. English. III. Title.
GN751. B27 2000 398.23'4—dc21 99-27943

ISBN 0-8050-6334-X
First American Edition 2000

Printed in Hong Kong

10 9 8 7 6 5 4 3 2

ATLANTIS

THE LEGEND OF A LOST CITY

Adapted and retold by CHRISTINA BALIT

With a note by Geoffrey Ashe

Henry Holt and Company • New York

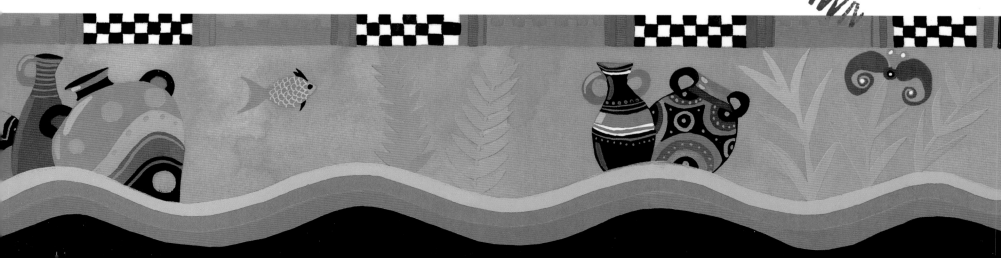

First there was Chaos.
From Chaos sprang Earth and Heaven.
From them came the race of Titans; two of
them, Cronus and Rhea, seized power and
ruled over all. Their son Zeus overthrew
them. Then he and his brothers divided up
the world: to Zeus went the heavens, to
Hades, the realms of the dead, while the seas
and oceans went to mighty Poseidon, who
promised to guard the waters with care.

Floating on one of Poseidon's emerald seas was a small rocky island. Few visited its shores and no one bothered to give it a name. But the sun rose warmly over it each morning and set sleepily behind it every night.

IN THE CENTER of the island there stood a mountain, and at the foot of the mountain lived a man called Evenor and his wife, Leucippe. They lived happily together, working hard to tend the barren land, and brought up their daughter Cleito to honor all creatures.

Poseidon grew curious. How could they be content with so little? He took on human form and crouched unseen behind a rock to find out.

Each morning at daybreak, he watched Cleito walk over the pebbled ground, barefoot and smiling, to fill her water pot at the stream.

EEING CLEITO in all her beauty, Poseidon's heart grew tender, and one day he stepped out from behind the rock to talk to her. Day after day he came and slowly she began to return his love. Finally she agreed to become his bride. Her parents, unaware of Poseidon's divinity, blessed the union, and a simple wedding followed.

But a god cannot stay hidden. After the wedding, all the spirits of the sea rose to the surface to sing, and Poseidon assumed his divine form once more. He vowed to rebuild the island and make it fit for a king and his queen.

POSEIDON used powers beyond human imagining to transform the isle into a paradise.

First, he arranged alternate circles of land and sea—three of land and three of water—to enclose the mountain. Within each circle of land a forest sprang up. Trees bloomed and grew heavy with fruits, and creatures multiplied.

Next, he made a network of canals, fed by waterfalls. Soon the island was yielding two crops each year—one watered by winter rains, the other irrigated by Poseidon's canals. The rich earth was carpeted with herbs and vegetables, and thick with healing roots; from its depths men dug out priceless yellow mountain copper. All things flourished on the sacred island.

THEN, under Poseidon's guidance, the inhabitants built a palace fit for a god, with towers, gates, and parapets trimmed with gleaming brass and tin. In the center they set up a holy temple dedicated to Poseidon and Cleito, with pinnacles of silver surrounded by a wall of gold.

They built thermal baths and aqueducts, fountains and gardens—and even a huge racecourse.

IT WAS A HAPPY TIME for Poseidon and Cleito, and over the years Cleito gave birth to five pairs of twin sons. Their firstborn son they named Atlas. In the summer of his twentieth year he was crowned high king, and they named the island Atlantis in his honor.

Then Poseidon divided the island into ten parts, and gave his sons one-tenth each.

 To ENSURE PEACE in his new island city, Poseidon set down laws in stone on a pillar of the temple. Chief among them was the commandment that no person should take up arms against another—with a terrible curse on anyone who disobeyed. Every five years, Atlas and the nine princes gathered by night beside the pillar to judge their people according to Poseidon's laws. The people of Atlantis became wise, gentle, and great-spirited. They were sober and kind, as the Creator had always wanted them to be. Above all, they lived in peace.

SO ATLANTIS prospered. Its splendid docks were thronged with ships and merchandise, and behind them, a towering lighthouse lit the way for incoming boats bringing cargoes from other lands. The harbors hummed with trade. Bridges and an underground canal were built to connect the three circles of land around the mountain, as the people grew ever richer.

Poseidon, watching from the waves, was content, and went away to his home at the bottom of the sea.

MANY years passed, and Poseidon lay sleeping at the bottom of the ocean. The people of Atlantis began to change. Slowly, very slowly, the godlike part of their souls faded and their mortal, human natures took over. They started to argue. Gradually they lost the gift of goodness and became infected with ambition and power. Greed filled the citizens' hearts. The streets of Atlantis, once safe, became dangerous, as people began to steal, cheat, and lie.

 ONE DAY ZEUS, god of gods, who ruled according to the law of the Creator, looked down from the heavens above. He saw the city walls crumbling with neglect, the empty temple, and, worst of all, people fighting one another. He roared out his anger.

The sound of his fury woke Poseidon. Rising to the surface of the waves, the sea-god looked out over his once-perfect kingdom— and wept.

Now he had no choice: he must carry out his terrible curse.

RAISING his trident, he stirred the seas into a wave that rose so high, it lashed the heavens. The wave vibrated with a roar that could be heard two thousand miles away, and the earth trembled in terror. Gathering its full force, the wave crashed upon the land, while burning rain and ashes blistered down from above.

In a single day and night, Atlantis was swallowed up by the sea.

 THEN there was silence. The city sank slowly to its new resting place on the ocean floor.

The people of Atlantis did not die. They continued to exist beneath the waves, but they never spoke or quarreled or fought again. As year followed year they paid a terrible penance, learning to live without gold or possessions in the cold depths. In time, they became little more than creatures of the water.

To this day, Atlantis has never been found. Some people believe that it is still there, under the sea, waiting to be discovered. . . .

WHERE WAS ATLANTIS?

People have suggested many different places where Atlantis might once have been. The oldest Greek legends describe Atlantis as being out to the west, in the middle of the ocean—the ocean that is still named the Atlantic, after Cleito's son. The people of Atlantis are said to have spread to other countries, founding settlements in Europe and Africa, and even in a land we now call America.

Some think Atlantis existed more or less as Plato described it, and that its people left traces behind them. Egypt has pyramids, Mexico has pyramids, so perhaps the Atlantean settlers built them in both places and their submerged homeland was midway between the two countries.

Others suggest that Atlantis was closer to America. The native inhabitants of the West Indies told early explorers that their islands were once part of a single landmass but that a disaster long ago shattered it. The fifth-century Greek philosopher Proclus, who wanted to convince his readers that Atlantis was real, writes, very mysteriously, as if he knew of the West Indies and their story.

Some people suggest that Atlantis was a part of Britain. Legend tells of a sunken land between Cornwall and the Isles of Scilly.

The theory taken most seriously is that the story is actually about the island of Crete, which was highly civilized and ruled over several smaller islands. One of them, Thera, was partially destroyed in about 1450 B.C.E. by a tremendous eruption, which also destroyed part of Crete, and its civilization never recovered.

With so much uncertainty, some argue that the story of Atlantis is not history at all but a myth warning us against conflict and power seeking. Yet the legend is so vivid that many will always believe Atlantis existed . . . somewhere.

Geoffrey Ashe